The Pony with the Bandaged Ear

Emma wasn't quite sure what she expected to see as the pony emerged from behind the bushes. Slowly and cautiously, she edged into view. Emma let out a sigh as first the head and then the rest of the body appeared. The pony stepped very apprehensively towards her.

"Tuppence!" gasped Emma. "You must be the most *beautiful* pony I have *ever* set eyes on."

The Pony with the Bandaged Ear

Brenda Jobling

SCHOLASTIC

For Beth Jessica Norman

Scholastic Children's Books,
Commonwealth House, 1–19 New Oxford Street,
London, WC1A 1NU, UK
a division of Scholastic Ltd
London ~ New York ~ Toronto ~ Sydney ~ Auckland
Mexico City ~ New Delhi ~ Hong Kong

First published in the UK by Scholastic Ltd, 2000

Copyright © Brenda Jobling, 2000
Cover illustration copyright © Mike Rowe, 2000

ISBN 0 439 99338 5

Typeset by M Rules
Printed by Cox & Wyman Ltd, Reading, Berks.

10 9 8 7 6 5 4 3 2 1

Chapter 1

"Stay at Uncle Tim's animal sanctuary for a week! When do we go?" said Emma, jumping up, eager to get packed.

"Hey, hold your horses, little sister," Jack laughed. "You'll need to ask Mum and Dad first. They might have other plans for you over half-term."

"Well, there's no time like now to ask them," said Emma, dashing off to the kitchen to see her parents.

Emma Hodges was fourteen. For as long as she could remember she had wanted to be a vet, just like her dad, the owner of Handley Road Veterinary Clinic in North London. Emma and her family lived in a big, old house, the ground floor of which had been converted to make the clinic. Emma couldn't wait to be old enough to go to veterinary college, like her brother Jack, providing she got the qualifications. At weekends and during school holidays she helped at the clinic by showing the patients and their owners into her dad's surgery. She loved the job. Being around animals was what Emma liked to do most of all.

"Look, Emma," said Dad, smiling. "If we let you go to the Peak District, you must remember the reason Jack is up there staying with Aunty Margaret and Uncle Tim. He's going for some work experience with the farming community. He'll be helping out a local vet, so you'll have to keep yourself occupied. Uncle Tim and Aunty Margaret are usually rushed off their feet too, especially when they have a lot of animals in."

"In that case they might appreciate a bit of help from me. Maybe that's why they've *invited* me!" Emma beamed.

"Just make sure you take a couple of thick fleeces," Mum advised. "It can get so cold up there."

"Does that mean I can go?" said Emma, giving Mum and Dad her most appealing look. Mr and Mrs Hodges looked at one another, then nodded in agreement.

"YES!" Emma shouted, jumping up and punching the air before rushing off to pack.

Jack popped his head around Emma's bedroom door.

"I take it from the look on your face, and the speed you're moving, that I'm to have my grotty little sister for company. Doesn't seem fair, really – I battle with the cattle in the Peaks, while you get to cuddle hedgehogs and foxcubs."

"Listen, you're lucky to have *anyone* for company on the journey up there. It's not exactly a bundle of first-class travelling fun in that old heap you call a car." Emma laughed, waiting for her brother to explode.

"Old heap! How *dare* you! I'll have you know Daisy and I have had a long and happy relationship since I rescued her from the scrapyard," Jack said defensively. "Daisy and me – we go well together!"

Emma skipped over to Jack and ruffled his thick mop of curly, red hair.

"That's because you're both red and rusty on top!" she giggled and ran off.

"Well, *I* may not take offence at your remarks about my faithful old car, but Daisy might be a bit more sensitive about who rides in her," Jack called after her. "Hurry up and get packed – we leave in precisely one hour!"

"Peak District – here I come!" sang Emma as she searched her room for the old suitcase she had covered in all sorts of animal stickers.

"I just don't understand. Daisy has *never* overheated before," sighed Jack, stroking his chin and leaving great oily smears on his face.

"Half an hour we've been parked here by the roadside with the bonnet up. Face facts," said Emma, staring at the engine in confusion. "Old Daisy's blood pressure is way up and she's leaking oil. If you want *my* opinion she's on the way out."

"Never!" said Jack defiantly. "I've fixed the oil problem. Now we just need to let the old girl cool down a bit. Anyway, if *you* want *my* opinion she didn't like you insulting her. I told you she's sensitive. She's just letting us know. Daisy will be fine in an hour or so. Now, make yourself useful and break out the sandwiches Mum packed. I need calories and there's enough cheese in those things to feed the entire mouse population of the British Isles. And get Uncle Tim on the mobile, too. Let him know we're running a bit late."

"Yes, sir!" laughed Emma, saluting Jack. "Anything else I can do while you just stand there? Shall I find a cow and milk it, perhaps, so you can have fresh milk for your coffee?"

"No, I don't think that will be necessary. Just the carton will do. Anyway, you don't know how to milk a cow – do you?"

Emma huddled next to Jack in the front of the old car. She felt very cold as they finished off the sandwiches and watched the last patch of sky change from day to night.

"Daisy must have cooled down by now. *I* certainly have. I've got more fleeces on my back than a flock of sheep and I'm *still* cold." Emma blew on her hands to warm them.

Jack pulled back his sleeves, like a magician,

and deftly turned the ignition key. Immediately, the old car sparked into life, as though it had suddenly shaken itself awake from a deep sleep.

"See!" said Jack, a huge smile breaking over his oil-streaked face. "Take it back – all the horrible stuff you said about my lovely little car. A bit of tender loving care and good old Daisy does the business for us." He grinned from ear to ear. "Now – let's hit the road, sister! I need some proper food inside me and I just bet Aunty Margaret has something really tasty waiting for us."

Two hours later, Emma and Jack pulled into a long winding track. A sign, with a squirrel in one corner and a foxcub in the other, said Little Woods Animal Sanctuary. The track led to a small house where Aunty Margaret and Uncle Tim lived. Around the house were a cluster of sheds and outbuildings. Emma remembered how Uncle Tim had converted them into shelters for all the creatures brought to him. Since retiring he had devoted himself to caring for wild animals. Many of them he helped heal, but others he'd watched slowly slip away and die. He often felt it was the best thing, if there was little chance of proper recovery from their injuries. Uncle Tim found the most difficult part of his job was comforting the children who brought him birds. Usually they had been caught by a cat or knocked by a car. Despite their injuries they often looked bright-eyed and alert. But Uncle Tim knew the signs and when the children phoned the next day, he usually had to report that the bird had died. Shock, puncture wounds and infection had given them a slim chance of survival. So he always tried hard to convince the children that they had done all they possibly could to help.

"Jack – Emma! Come on in and warm yourselves. You poor things must be cold and starving!" Uncle Tim called from the porch. Emma thought he was a welcome sight standing silhouetted against the warm glow from the farmhouse.

"You're right, Uncle," Emma smiled as the big man hugged her. Straight away she recalled how he always wore thick, woolly jumpers that smelled of fresh air, straw and animals.

"How you've grown!" said Uncle Tim.

"Me too?" laughed Jack, reaching out to shake Uncle Tim's big, callused hand.

Emma felt warm and cosy the minute she set foot in the big old kitchen. Aunty Margaret greeted her with more hugs and the biggest dish of vegetarian lasagne Emma had ever seen.

"Ooh, yummy!" said Jack. But Emma had seen that his expression didn't quite match his words. Jack loved his meat dishes and he'd forgotten Uncle Tim and Aunty Margaret were vegetarians.

Emma held out her plate for a third helping of home-grown rhubarb and apple crumble with lashings of creamy custard.

"Tell me about the animals you have in at the moment, Uncle," she asked.

"Well, I've almost lost count, but let me think," he said, scratching his head. "Yes, we have a badger with a leg injury, two rabbits that were probably hit by cars, but not too badly. Then, there are assorted birds, like wood pigeons and blackbirds. They're mostly road-accident victims, too. There's a kestrel and, of course, we still have old Bessie, the barn owl with one wing. Do you remember her, Emma? She's a permanent resident here. She wouldn't survive long outside the sanctuary. But she seems quite content in her shelter, just dozing or watching what goes on around her."

Emma could see her uncle's eyes light up as he spoke with enthusiasm about the wild creatures.

"We have the most beautiful vixen – a really lovely fox, found at the side of the road by a lady. I think the fox had been stunned a bit by a passing car. She's still limping a little, but nothing so serious that we can't let her go in a few days. Oh, yes, and you'll like this, Emma. How would you like to help feed two orphaned baby hedgehogs in the morning?"

"Baby hedgies – how sweet," Emma cooed. "I'd love to help."

"Well," said Jack, rubbing his tummy. "That

pudding was delicious, Aunty Margaret. I think I just need to chill out in front of your fire, before getting my beauty sleep. Tomorrow morning, I'm filling in for the vet I'm up here to assist – the poor man has taken an emergency call that could last all night. So, it's a cow at the Bruntons' farm for my first call. That's no problem for *this* vet in training."

"Whatever it is, the Bruntons must be worried if they're calling a vet out," said Uncle Tim. "They're a miserable old pair who live up at Windy Ridge Farm with their grand-daughter. I went up there once. The whole place could do with a clean up, if you ask me."

Emma saw Uncle Tim looking concerned as he spoke. She watched Jack plod out of the kitchen followed by Jason, Bess and Samson. They were the three stray dogs Uncle Tim and Aunty Margaret had taken in over the years.

"They'll curl up asleep on the end of his bed given half the chance," laughed Aunty Margaret.

"No wonder they're called hogs – hedgehogs, I mean. They are *so* greedy. Look at this little fella." Emma laughed as she squeezed the feeder, a little pipette that the tiny bundle of life was emptying at the other end.

Uncle Tim smiled. "I'm going to rub them with a little baby oil when they've had enough."

"Baby oil!" laughed Emma. "You'll be telling me next that you've got disposable nappies for them."

"Not quite, but they do need a lot of looking after without their mum around. The oil and massage is like their mother licking them. It stimulates their circulation and they need that to be in working order to keep warm."

Emma and Uncle Tim eventually put the sleepy baby hedgehogs back in their box. Emma watched as they snuggled into the old jumper wrapped around a warm hot-water bottle.

"How would you like to help me put out food for the other animals?" asked Uncle Tim.

"I'd love to, Uncle, but Jack said I could go with him to the Bruntons' farm. I've never been on a real working farm before and, if I'm going to be a vet, well, I might just decide to specialize in livestock like Jack."

"All right, Emma, but stay close to him. They don't take too kindly to strangers up at Windy Ridge Farm," warned Uncle Tim.

As Jack drove his little car into the farmyard, Emma pinched her nose and screwed her face up.

"Yuk! What a stink!" she squealed. "I think I'll stick to Dad's type of veterinary work and look after domestic animals. This place is much too smelly!"

"This place doesn't seem to be a good advertisement for a farm at all," said Jack. "It's true they pong a bit, but Uncle Tim is right, Windy Ridge Farm could do with a clean up. Look at all that rotting old muck lying around the farmyard."

"Are you *sure* this is the right place? I didn't see a sign on the gate. It gives me the creeps, Jack. I'm sure it's deserted," said Emma, feeling uncomfortable.

Emma stared at the crumbling brickwork, full of weeds growing from the cracks. She took in the piles of rotting feed boxes stacked outside a front door that looked as if it was locked tight. She noticed the windows had a yellow tinge to them, as though they hadn't been cleaned for years. A scrawny cockerel suddenly fluttered up on to the bonnet of Jack's car. It thrust its little beady eyes close to the windscreen and let out a cry that made Emma jump.

"Hey! Mind the paintwork!" called Jack, banging on the windscreen.

"Come on, Jack, let's get out of here," said Emma, frowning. "This place is weird. Only rats and ghosts live here, I reckon."

Emma caught her breath and gasped when Jack suddenly grabbed her arm and pointed to one of the windows. She looked up and saw that a grey curtain had been pulled aside. A dark figure lurked behind it. Jack's eyes were wide open and staring.

"*Aaah*! Look, Em! There's one of the ghosts now!"

Chapter 2

"You are *so* unfunny, Jack!" shouted Emma, pushing her brother out of the car. "You *really* frightened me then!"

She followed him towards the tall, thin man who had started to walk out of the farmhouse.

"Mr Brunton," smiled Jack, offering the man his hand. "Mr West, your vet, has sent me to cover for him. He's been up most of the night on an emergency call."

Emma noticed the unshaven man in grubby blue overalls didn't extend his hand to return the greeting. Instead, he eyed Jack suspiciously from beneath heavy, dark eyebrows.

"Bit young for a vet, aren't you? You know what you're doing?" he demanded.

"I'm almost qualified," replied Jack. "I really don't think Mr West would have asked me to take a look at your cow if he didn't think I was up to the job, do you?"

Emma watched Jack and thought how hard he was trying to remain polite with the rude farmer. But the man just scowled.

"Of course, I could go and you can wait until Mr West is available. But if you're worried about your cow, then perhaps it's best if I take a look at her?" Jack smiled.

Emma was just deciding she really didn't like the grumpy man when he suddenly announced, "I'll take you to her – she's in the barn!"

As Emma followed her brother and Mr Brunton into the barn, she struggled to accustom her eyes to the dark. She had thought the smell in the yard was bad enough, but found the stench inside the gloomy building even worse. A big brown and white cow stood tethered facing the wall in a cramped stall.

"She's so sweet. What's her name?" Emma enquired.

"Name – what name? She's just one of my cows. Who are you then, his assistant?" snapped Mr Brunton.

"No, I'm his sister. I hope to be a vet one day. My brother said I could come with him today to see a real working farm." Emma tried to appear friendly.

"Not much room for you in here," mumbled the man.

"I'll just get some fresh air then, Jack, while you examine Mr Brunton's cow," Emma said, taking Mr Brunton's hint and pleased at the chance to go outside again.

"Don't *touch* anything," scowled the man. "Lot of expensive farm equipment around here."

Emma strolled out into the light and took a deep breath. She even felt relieved to smell the odour of the yard after the rotting barn. She felt even more pleased she'd escaped the horrible atmosphere that surrounded Mr Brunton like a fog. Emma decided that the expensive farm equipment she'd been told to stay away from looked like a lot of rusting, old hulks of metal.

"I've no intention of going anywhere near that dangerous old junk," she said to herself. Wandering around the back of the barn, she found a muddy field. Emma pricked up her ears when she heard a girl's voice coming from behind a clump of bushes.

"I really don't know *why* I bother riding you, Tuppence. You're just no fun any more!"

Emma was curious. "Who is Tuppence?" she muttered, tiptoeing over to find out more. A short, slim girl appeared from behind the bushes. She was carrying a small saddle and bridle in her arms. She stopped in her tracks when she saw Emma.

"What do *you* want?" she snapped. "You're on private property, you know."

Despite the frosty greeting, Emma forced herself to smile.

"I realize that, and I'm sorry if I made you jump. I'm here with my brother; he's a vet. He's come to have a look at one of the cows."

Emma supposed this was the Bruntons' granddaughter, who'd obviously inherited her unfriendly attitude from her grandparents. She moved swiftly to open the gate for her. The girl pushed past without thanking Emma.

"Is Tuppence your horse – or perhaps your pony, looking at the size of that saddle?" said Emma, trying to peer around the bushes for any trace of the animal the girl had just dismounted. The girl stopped and turned.

"She's my pony – and if you're looking for her, you probably *won't* see her. She's too nervous for my liking. Used to be a good ride, but she's past her best."

Emma could feel her face flushing. She felt angry that the girl had spoken about her pony as though she was nothing better than a piece of machinery, fit only to serve her.

"Are you giving her any water after your ride?" Emma asked.

"There's a trough at the other end of the field," the girl called over her shoulder as she walked away. "She knows where it is."

"What a *lovely* family," Emma mumbled to herself as she shut the gate. She climbed on the first bar to look in the direction of the bushes again, hoping to catch sight of the pony.

"Come on, Tuppence!" she called. "Let's have a look at you."

At first there was no movement, so Emma repeated her call. Eventually, the bushes stirred. "Tuppence," she said. "Come on, girl. Come and see me."

Emma wasn't quite sure what she expected to see as the pony emerged from behind the bushes. Slowly and cautiously, she edged into view. Emma let out a sigh as first the head and then the rest of the body appeared. The pony stepped very apprehensively towards her.

"Tuppence!" gasped Emma. "You must be the most *beautiful* pony I have *ever* set eyes on."

A thin, dark brown pony with the biggest dark brown eyes Emma had ever seen, on any creature, plodded towards her. When the pony reached the gate she lifted her head and rested it over the top. Emma studied the gentle face. She looked at the pony's big, appealing eyes and saw they were veiled by long black eyelashes.

"You *are* a beauty!" she said, reaching cautiously to stroke the pony's neck so as not to frighten her away. "But what's *this*?" Emma cried, gently touching one of the pony's ears. "What on earth has happened to your poor ear?" Emma winced as she looked closely at the ear. She saw it was torn a bit at the top and thought it was an old wound that had healed that way. But further down, her fingers touched a grubby bandage, tied too tightly, over another injury. Emma felt herself melting as the pony blinked her big, dark lashes and rubbed her neck on the gate.

"Got an itch, Tuppence? Here, let me scratch it for you – poor thing," she whispered. Emma looked to see any sign of the Bruntons' granddaughter. "I feel like giving your owner a piece of my mind," she said, stroking the side of Tuppence's head.

Emma thought the pony seemed to like the attention she was giving her. But she felt sad when her hands made contact with the thick matted coat, covered in clumps of dried mud, on Tuppence's neck.

"They've really neglected you," she said, turning her attention to the tangled mane that stuck together in dirty hanks. But Emma felt most troubled when she realized how thin and undernourished the pony's body felt beneath her hands. "If you were mine I'd give you the best feed I could afford and the sweetest pasture to graze in. I'd brush you too, until you shone."

Tuppence leaned her beautiful head further over the fence and nearer to Emma, but suddenly shot it back when a loud shout split the air. A bellow, like a moose in pain, erupted from the direction of the barn. Emma could see Tuppence was so startled that her eyes had widened and her ears had twitched in the direction of the sound. She had a sneaking feeling the sound had come from Jack.

"Steady, girl! You *are* nervous," Emma said, comforting Tuppence. She shooed away a fly that buzzed around the dirty bandage.

"*Arghh!*"

Emma heard the bellow again. This time she was convinced it was her brother. Once again, she saw Tuppence raise her head and flinch at the sound as she started to move away.

"Stay, Tuppence!" Emma said, trying to settle the pony. "I'll be back with my brother, just as soon as I've discovered what he's done to himself." Emma felt reluctant to leave her. She sighed as she ran. "Oh, Jack, however gifted you may be as a vet – you're more than just a bit accident-prone."

Jack sat on a low stool inside the dark, cobweb-filled barn. One trouser leg was rolled up and he'd taken off his sock and shoe. Emma looked at the painful expression on his face. She watched as he waved away an inquisitive hen with his sock as it tried to peck his big toe.

"Cow – trod – on – foot," he winced, his words coming in short puffs while he rubbed his foot. "Stepped – full weight on it! No bones broken – just bad bruises."

Emma noticed Mr Brunton standing gloomily in the shadows. She helped Jack replace his sock and shoe as the farmer glared impatiently.

"Well, Mr Brunton," said Jack, eventually able to stand by leaning on Emma for support. "I'll make sure the milk specimen I took gets to Mr West. He will probably want to come and take a look at the rest of your herd. I've given your cow something for her slight fever, too. Make sure you keep her comfortable and clean," he added, looking around and hoping the man would get the drift of his meaning.

Mr Brunton grunted and started to make his way back to the farmhouse.

"Jack," whispered Emma as she tied his shoelace. "I know you're in pain, but there's the most beautiful pony in a field behind the barn. She's thin and really neglected. Looks like she's got a cut on her ear, too. The tip is torn a bit, but healed up from an old wound. Now someone has tied a dirty old bandage around a new cut. Please say you'll take a look at her."

"Mr Brunton!" Jack called after the retreating figure. "My sister tells me your pony has an injury to her ear. Mind if I take a look?"

Mr Brunton turned, his dark features frowning in the light. "Do what you want as long as it won't cost me! That pony's always rubbing itself on wire. That's how she caught her ear the first time and split it. Got a new cut – I've done it up – shouldn't be a problem. Reckon we'll get rid of her soon. Belongs to my granddaughter – she's grown out of her now." Before he disappeared inside his front door he shouted. "Tell Mr West I'll pay *him* for the cow's treatment next time I see him!"

Emma watched open-mouthed as Mr Brunton slammed the front door. "Nice family!" she sighed. "I've already met the granddaughter. I think she must have graduated from the same school of charm as old Brunton."

"I'd really like to have told him to clean this *filthy* place up," Jack said angrily. "It's probably not helped his cow's condition, either. And he's obviously left it as long as possible before contacting the vet. I doubt if he ever wants to pay out for his animals and livestock, unless he really has to."

Emma watched as Jack put his full weight down on his foot. She thought it looked easier.

"Old Brunton wouldn't take kindly to any advice from me," continued Jack, "so I'll let Mr West know my opinion of this place. He can tell him to clean it up. Come on, sis. Let's have a look at the latest wounded creature you've found for me."

Emma was surprised to find Tuppence still standing where she'd left her, although the pony started to move away when she caught sight of Jack.

"Steady, girl!" cooed Emma. "This is my brother. He won't hurt you. He just wants to take a look at your ear."

Tuppence responded to Emma's voice by leaning her head over the gate.

"No wonder she's been rubbing herself on the wire fence," said Jack. "I don't think she's been brushed in months. She's a lovely little thing, but judging by her general state of health, I'd say she could do with some decent feed. As for pasture – this field is bald – only mud! You'd be hard pressed to find a blade of grass anywhere!" Jack concluded, shaking his head in disapproval.

"Just keep her head steady while I remove this bandage, Em," he asked. "Old Brunton has tied it too tightly around her ear. I suppose he thought he was doing some good. If she caught it on dirty wire though, she should have had an injection against tetanus."

Emma stroked the side of Tuppence's lovely dark head while Jack quickly, but gently, removed the bandage.

"Hmm," he said, when he'd finished, without Tuppence moving once or seeming too afraid. "It looks a lot worse than it is, Em. Thankfully it's not deep and there's no sign of infection. But I'm going to give her a tetanus injection just to make sure she's covered."

Before Jack prepared the syringe, Emma watched him swab and clean the wound and area around it with an antiseptic wash. Taking care not to alarm Tuppence, Jack carefully cleared away all the crusted, dried blood.

"Look at her, Jack. She's nodding off," Emma smiled. "You certainly have the Hodges touch with animals. They go all sleepy for Dad, too."

"Well, I must have lost my special touch with Mr Brunton's cow, seeing as she crushed every bone in my poor foot," he laughed. "We'll let some fresh air get to the cut. Now I've cleaned it there won't be too much trouble from flies. Hold her very steady, now, Em. I'm going to give her the jab."

The pony stood quietly as Jack slipped the needle into her neck. Her eyes only left Emma's face for a second when they swivelled to look at Jack as he spoke.

"All done, Tuppence!" he smiled, packing up his case. "I think I'll have a word with your owners and tell them what I've done. Make sure they get out here and give you some feed."

"Oh, Tuppence, I've got to leave you now, but I'll be back in a day or so to see you," said Emma, looking at her brother.

"Yes, Em, I get the hint. I can see you've really taken to her, and she likes you, too, by the look of it. Don't worry, we'll be back. I'll want to check that old Brunton has got the message about taking better care of her, especially feeding her."

Emma ran her hand down the pony's cheek and felt Tuppence's warm, sweet breath on her face. She breathed in deeply, drinking in the smell she loved best of all in the world – the smell of animals.

"I'll be thinking about you, Tuppence, until I see you again."

Emma walked alongside Jack as he limped his way back to the Bruntons' farmhouse. She thought the place looked even gloomier since the sky had turned grey and started to spit little flecks of rain on her face. Jack knocked firmly on the door. But there was no answer.

"I'm *sure* they're in," he said. "I didn't hear anyone leaving."

Emma looked up at one of the upstairs windows and noticed a curtain twitching.

"Look!" she whispered. "Someone's in, all right."

Jack knocked again, but still there was no reply. After waiting a few more minutes he produced a notebook and pen from his jacket, and dashed off a note. Emma watched as he stood back from the door. Staring up at the window where the curtain moved, very slightly, he said in a loud voice: "Right! As the *entire* Brunton family seems to be unavailable to answer, I will leave this note under the knocker on their front door! Let's hope they find the note – *under the knocker on their front door!*"

"Come on Jack, let's get out of here," said Emma, tugging at his sleeve. "I reckon they heard only too well. The farm in the next valley must have heard you shouting!"

Jack winced whenever he put his injured foot on the brake, as the little car wound its way around the track leading from the Bruntons' farm. Emma turned to look over her shoulder in the hope of seeing Tuppence once more.

"Jack," she sighed. "Tuppence is *still* there, leaning her head over the gate – just as we left her. I really think she liked us. I only wish they took more care of her and appreciated her."

"Well, if Mr Brunton gets the message I've left for him, he'll have to improve his attitude towards her."

As the little car wove its way through the country lanes that wriggled their way across the landscape, Emma looked around at the beautiful scenery.

"How can such a lovely place as this be home to those miserable Bruntons? Just look at it, Jack – rolling hills and lots of fluffy sheep, like clouds, everywhere. This is *so* different from where we live in town. I think I could get used to living here, you know. I can see it now – a cosy, country cottage, a couple of old dogs, a few cats – and Tuppence. She'd have her own stable and a field full of the sweetest grass to eat and roll in when she's tired."

"Stop day-dreaming, little sis. Life is hard up here, especially for the farmers. Imagine what it's like in winter, when you're snowed in, or the wind and rain sting your face so much it hurts." Jack smiled as he swung the car on to the track leading to his uncle's house. "Yes, being a vet in these parts is a tough job. It's a job that requires someone strong, dependable and hardened to all sorts of weather. Someone like me who is rugged, tough and afraid of nothing. . ."

Emma noticed Jack had suddenly broken off in mid-sentence, and his face had gone pale as he stared ahead. He hit the brake with his injured foot and painfully brought the car to a halt.

"Whatever is the *matter*, Jack!" Emma stared at her brother's profile as he seemed frozen to the spot. Parked in front of the house was a bright pink Mini.

". . . afraid of nothing," he continued, hurriedly attempting to start the car up again, but failing. "Nothing – but *Gloria Scrumbel!*"

Already Emma could see the front door of Uncle Tim's house opening and a tall, thin woman dashing out. She wore bright pink, tight-fitting leggings, a fluffy pink jumper covered in gold jewellery, and spiky high heels. She was waving frantically at them as she ran up the path.

"JACK! *JACK!* IT'S ME – GLORIA!"

Chapter 3

"**S**he can't be another one of your girlfriends you're trying to escape! You should stick to animals!" Emma watched the figure wobbling towards them. She saw her almost fall off her stiletto heels as they caught in the rutted track.

"Animals!" whispered Jack. "Gloria *is* an animal – and a hungry one who wants to get her claws into me for a husband! Come *on*, Daisy, don't play up now when I really need you!"

Emma tried not to laugh at Jack's frantic efforts to start the car. But she saw he had no hope of escaping Gloria. She was already bearing down on him through the window.

Emma smelled the scent of overpowering perfume wafting into the car. She could hear the clink of wrists laden with bracelets, too. In an instant, a hand with pink-painted talons reached in through Jack's window and squeezed his cheek.

"Jack, you *naughty* boy! For a moment there I thought you were trying to get away from me!" Gloria cooed, as Jack wriggled uncomfortably and forced a silly, embarrassed smile across his face.

"Get away from you, Gloria? Whatever gave you that idea?" he said.

"Margaret told me you were staying," Gloria purred. "So I simply left everything and dashed over, just as I was, to see you. Oh, dear, you must think me a *dreadful* mess. I didn't even have time to do my hair and make-up!"

Emma managed to turn a laugh into a cough as she ran her gaze over the woman's face. She thought it threatened to subside at any moment under the weight of foundation, mascara and lipstick.

"Don't tell me," Gloria said, turning her attention to Emma. "This must be your little sister. Those good looks of yours certainly run in the family, Jack."

Emma watched Jack try to make a dash for it while Gloria's attention was on her for a moment.

"Well, Gloria," he said. "It's so nice to see you again, but I really must be getting inside now. Got an urgent phone call to make to Mr West, the vet I'm assisting." Jack heaved himself out of the driving seat and winced as his painful foot touched the ground.

"You poor darling!" Gloria almost swooned. "You're hurt! Here, let me help you into the house."

Emma put her hand over her mouth to stifle the giggles forcing their way out. She watched as Gloria coiled herself around Jack like a fluffy, pink snake and gripped him tightly around the waist.

"That's right, Jack! Lean all your weight on me!" Gloria insisted.

Emma picked up Jack's bag and joined the strange procession down the path. When Jack looked over his shoulder at her, she thought his eyes showed real terror, as though a grizzly bear had him in her grip. Emma smiled and mouthed, silently: "You make a *lovely* couple!"

"Just look at him sitting there all pampered, wrapped in a blanket with his foot up on cushions," laughed Emma. "He's always got some poor woman running around after him," she said, watching Gloria's pink Mini rumble off down the track. Emma had tried not to laugh when Gloria had insisted on massaging Jack's foot with the baby oil Uncle Jack used to massage the baby hedgehogs.

"Well, in this case, he didn't need to encourage Gloria to run around after him," said Uncle Tim, defending Jack. "Gloria Scrumbel has always had a reputation for running after any single men. She lives in hope of trapping an unwary victim – a suitable candidate for marriage. You see, potential husbands are a bit thin on the ground in these remote parts. So when a single, handsome and available young vet appears on the scene, she can't wait to march him up the aisle." Uncle Tim laughed at the thought.

"Uncle, you *can't* be serious. She's twice his

age," Emma responded, her eyes wide in amazement.

"*She's* serious, all right. Gloria would drag Jack to the altar tomorrow, given half the chance. With him limping, too! She's always liked our Jack."

"Please feel free to talk about me while I sit here trussed up like a prize turkey at Christmas! Thank you so much for coming to my rescue, Emma. Don't think I couldn't hear you giggling in the kitchen, while that she-wolf tried to get her talons into me!"

Jack began unwrapping himself from the blanket Gloria had wound tightly around him. Emma thought he looked like a moth emerging from a chrysalis as he struggled.

"I'm going to make a call to Mr West now, and tell him of my findings at the Bruntons' farm. Then, I'm going to take a long warm bath. I want to wash away that awful pong of Gloria's perfume. If that nightmare in pink phones to see how her patient is doing, tell her I've had an urgent call-out to an African safari park. And I *won't* be coming back!"

*

Uncle Tim made Emma a cup of hot chocolate and asked her about the trip up to Windy Ridge Farm.

"You were right about them being a miserable lot, but it's not them that I'm concerned about, it's the granddaughter's lovely pony, Tuppence. She's been badly neglected. Nobody seemed bothered by a nasty cut on her ear, either. Jack has given her an injection against tetanus, but it should have been done when she cut it. They shouldn't have just left it. I mean, it's not that anyone has deliberately ill-treated her, more that no one seems to care about her."

"I told you they were a strange lot up there. Most of the farmers who live around here are very friendly and get on well together. But Mr Brunton, well, he doesn't want anything to do with the rest of the community." Uncle Tim smiled. "Don't worry, Emma, if Jack's picked up on any problem he'll sort it out, providing he isn't escaping from the clutches of Gloria Scrumbel."

That night Emma woke up from a dream. She

stared at her unfamiliar surroundings and slowly remembered where she was staying – a long way from her bed, back home in North London.

"That was horrible!" she said, getting up to look out of the window. The early morning light was spreading across the field at the back of the house. But the dream still seemed very real and she couldn't get it out of her mind. In it, Mr Brunton had led Tuppence away down a long, misty lane. No matter how fast she'd run, she just couldn't catch up with them.

"I might as well get up and take a look at those baby hedgehogs," she said, pulling on her dressing gown. "They'll take my mind off worrying about Tuppence. Uncle Tim is right; Jack will make sure she gets proper care."

Emma thought the kitchen was such a friendly place. The old-fashioned cooking range warmed every corner of the room. She loved the smell of Aunty Margaret's home-baked bread, too. It always filled the air, even when she wasn't baking. Emma padded silently through the kitchen on her way to the conservatory, where the baby hedgehogs snuggled together. She stopped for a drink of water, letting the clear, cold stream gush into her glass from the tap. Then she guzzled it thirstily. Before leaving the kitchen Emma pulled up the blind to let the morning light flood in. But as it rolled upwards, and Emma looked out, she found herself staring straight into the face of a man peering into the window.

"*Uncle!*" Emma screamed, rushing out of the room and dashing upstairs.

"Hey! Steady there!" said Uncle Tim as Emma collided with him coming out of the bathroom.

"Oh, Uncle! There's a man staring in at the kitchen window. Quick! Go downstairs and catch him! *Come on!*"

Uncle Tim smiled. "It's all right, Emma. Did he have a big old cap on and look as though he's in need of a bit of a shave?" he asked.

Emma looked confused. "Yes, he did, *why?*"

"I'm so sorry, Emma," apologized Uncle Tim. "I should have told you about Fred. He's quite harmless, but he must have given you a nasty shock. He's a friend who just turns up for spare food for all his animals. If you've recovered from your shock, come and meet him."

Emma followed Uncle Tim downstairs and stood by while he unbolted the back door.

"Hello, Fred. You gave my niece here quite a fright. I should have told her that you're always the first one up in these parts. Come on in and I'll put the kettle on."

Emma watched the tall man step shyly into the room and remove his cap. She also saw that something in his old overcoat pocket was moving. He spoke, without looking up to meet her gaze.

"I'm so sorry. Didn't mean to scare you. I always knock on the back window – usually find your uncle or aunty here, at this time. They're early birds, like me. I have to be up for the animals, you see."

"That's all right," replied Emma. "I think I was in a jumpy sort of mood. I'd just woken up from a bad dream. You know how it is." She smiled, still looking at the wriggling pocket.

Fred followed her gaze. "Oh, my coat. No need to be afraid. It's a baby field mouse. I found her on the path on the way over – just lying there. I'm keeping her safe and warm until I get her home and take a proper look at her. I think she'll make it."

"Fred has quite a way with animals, Emma," said Uncle Tim. "He takes them in when they're wounded, just like me and your Aunty Margaret. Except he lives in a caravan, in the woods, at the bottom of our field. Some of his creatures have recovered when I'd have given up hope. You've got a way with them, haven't you, Fred?"

Fred looked embarrassed and spoke modestly.

"You just have to be quiet around them and real patient. I've got plenty of time, these days," he said.

Emma thought Fred had a far-away look in his eyes as he said that. She watched Uncle Tim hand him a mug of tea and offer a plate of biscuits.

"Do you need food for those hungry old dogs of yours?" he asked. "Fred has five dogs, Emma, all strays he's given a home – a good home. He's got an old crow, too. He nursed that back to health as well. Only thing is, once the bird was well it decided to stay – liked Fred's company too much. It lives in the caravan with him, now. That old bird isn't stupid – it couldn't have a nicer, cosier home."

Fred looked up and Emma could see he seemed suddenly distressed.

"That's what I came to see you about. It won't be my home for much longer." He reached inside his coat and pulled out a bundle of papers. "Got these delivered to me last evening. They're eviction notices. They say I'm a health hazard because of all the animals and I've got to go."

"Health hazard, my foot!" exclaimed Uncle Tim. "That's just something they've cooked up to get you off the land. There's probably some investors behind this who've got their eye on land near the woods."

"I just wondered whether you would take the animals – just the ones that still need caring for, and the old crow. Don't want to make a fuss or anything. I'll just take the dogs and go. We'll be all right," Fred said, swigging back his tea and getting up to go.

"Of course I'll have them. But leave it with me, Fred. I may be able to come up with something better. I don't know what, but it seems so wrong that you should be evicted after all the time you've been there."

Emma watched Uncle Tim studying the papers and although his voice sounded hopeful she could see he looked concerned.

Fred left as silently as he'd appeared at the window. Emma felt a great wave of sympathy for him sweep over her.

"Poor old Fred. He's a sad case, Emma," said Uncle Tim. "He lost his young wife, years ago, and just never got over it. Since then he's lived in those woods. All that love he had for her, well, it just goes into caring for the wild creatures, now. As for being a health hazard – rubbish! Fred's place and his animal pens are spotless."

"Will you be able to help him, Uncle Tim?" Emma asked.

"I just don't know. Fred's a loner. I'm not sure he could ever settle down anywhere. What a shame to lose such a lovely, caring person. I hope I can think of something to help. But I suppose as he doesn't own the land his caravan's on, then they can evict him for squatting. Hard to think of Fred as a squatter. He's always been there looking after the wild creatures – just giving them a helping hand."

"Well, I've been thinking about someone I can help today," said Emma. "If Jack can take me into the nearest town, I'm going to draw some money out of my building society account. I won't feel peaceful until I've provided Tuppence with some nourishing feed. I want to get her a few other bits and pieces to help improve her condition, too. A decent brush to groom her, for a start!" Emma ended defiantly.

"Emma, that's much too generous and it won't be appreciated by the Bruntons. In fact, I can imagine old Brunton telling you his granddaughter's pony is none of your business," said Uncle Tim.

Emma's eyes flashed and Uncle Tim raised his eyebrows.

"Any animal is my business when I don't think it's getting treated properly!"

"Be careful, Emma. Let Jack handle the

Bruntons," Uncle Tim warned as he started to make up the feed for the hedgehogs.

An hour passed while Emma waited for Jack to wake up. She had helped Uncle Tim feed the baby hedgehogs again, and played with the dogs, Samson, Jason and Bess. They had followed Aunty Margaret downstairs into the kitchen.

"Still no sign of your brother rousing himself yet," Aunty Margaret said. "If he's going to work in a country practice eventually, he'll have to get up with the lark. I wish I hadn't let it slip to Gloria that he's staying, though. I don't think I'm his favourite aunt any longer."

"Thanks, Aunty Margaret," smiled Emma. "You've just given me an idea to get Jack up. Watch, I bet he's down those stairs in no time."

Emma crept noiselessly into Jack's room and over to his bed. She could see the wild, red curls spreading out over the pillow as she bent over him to whisper in his ear.

"Jack, how would you like to give me a lift into town on your way to see Mr West?"

Jack's voice crept out, muffled and sleepy, from beneath the duvet. "Go away, Em! I spoke to Mr West last night. I'm not needed until this afternoon. Kindly push off and let me go back to sleep!"

"Put it this way, Jack," Emma whispered. "It may be to your advantage to be out of the house today, if a certain lady named Gloria calls by. Don't forget, she did say *she'd be back!*"

Emma stepped backwards as Jack sat bolt upright and shrieked.

"Oh, no! Anything but another confrontation with that husband-hunter! Now clear off, Em, while I get dressed. I'll be ready to leave in half an hour."

Emma was impressed when, despite his injury, Jack was sitting in the car exactly thirty minutes later.

"If your foot is really playing up then don't go," said Emma. "I heard you howl as I shut your bedroom door and felt rotten for bothering you."

"No problem. It's feeling better all the time," said Jack, eager to move. "The sooner we're away from here, the better," he said as Daisy bumped along the track on the way to town.

On the way Emma explained why she wanted to withdraw her money.

"Are you bonkers? I should think that old skinflint, Brunton, will be only too pleased if you keep his granddaughter's pony supplied with feed. And you reckon you're going to buy a grooming kit for Tuppence, too. Stop worrying, sis, I'll take another look at the pony when I go back in a few days time. Hopefully, Mr West will be there. If there's been no improvement in Tuppence's condition, then we'll deal with it."

"I'm sorry, Jack, but I just have to do something now. I won't sleep easy until I know that I've made some effort for her." Jack knew Emma's stubborn streak only too well. It was pointless arguing.

Jack pulled the car into the kerb in town. Emma pointed across the road. "Look, there's a cash machine. I won't be a minute," she said.

"Right," said Jack. "But I don't want to hang about, just in case you-know-who is around, buying up another litre of perfume and something else pink and frilly to impress me."

Emma stood at the cash machine, waiting for it to deliver her hard-saved money from its mouth. A horsebox drawing up at the traffic lights close by caught her eye.

"Thank you," she said as the machine delivered four new ten-pound notes into her hand. As she took them, she glanced up at the driver of the horsebox. "Mr Brunton!" she gasped, anxious to see what was in the back of the vehicle. As he pulled away when the lights changed, she felt sure he'd seen her, and as the back of the vehicle came into view Emma gasped again.

"Tuppence! Where is he taking you!"

Emma felt her legs go wobbly as she caught a glimpse of the lovely dark head and sad eyes. Then Mr Brunton accelerated and Tuppence was driven away – out of reach.

"Quick, Jack! Let's go!" Emma called, banging Daisy's roof and startling her brother.

"Oh, no!" said Jack, desperately flicking on the ignition.

Emma leapt into the passenger seat. "She's in the back of that horsebox. Goodness knows where old Brunton's taking her, but we can't lose them in the traffic. Just follow them, Jack!"

Jack drove off, his eyes starting from his head. "Why on earth would Mr Brunton put her in a horsebox? Perhaps they're running away together. I don't want to hang around to find out – I should be happy, Emma! Why don't we just let them go?"

Emma felt confused. "What *are* you talking about? Why are you so pleased Mr Brunton is driving Tuppence away the *very next day* after we saw her!"

Jack breathed out slowly.

"You twit, Emma. You should have said it was Tuppence! I thought you were talking about Gloria!"

Emma and Jack drove for less than half a mile when the traffic lights changed and they had to stop. Emma felt frustrated as she saw the horsebox gaining distance.

"Oh no! We're going to lose them now, Jack. Look, they're way ahead, following the road out of town. Where do you think he could be taking her?"

Chapter 4

"It's anyone's guess what old Brunton has in mind," sighed Jack. "But I really can't imagine he's developed a sudden interest in entering his granddaughter's pony for a gymkhana, or best-kept pony show, in her condition. I'm sorry to say it, but I wouldn't mind betting there will be money in it for him somewhere."

"Can't Daisy go any *faster*!" said Emma, straining her eyes as she looked for the horsebox.

"Sorry, sis. Daisy's top speed isn't much above forty – and that's on one of her good days. She'll blow a gasket if I push her any harder."

As they left the town behind and headed out on open road Emma wriggled in her seat and bit her fingernails. She kept her eyes fixed on the road, unable to get the image of Tuppence out of her mind.

"I *know* they're up ahead, but it's impossible to see beyond this big lorry that's pulled in front of us," she sighed.

Emma breathed a sigh of relief as the lorry eventually turned off and she suddenly had a clear view ahead.

"We've *lost* them, Jack! I can't see them anywhere!"

"Well, Mr Brunton couldn't have been driving too fast if he's trailing a horsebox. He must have turned down a side road or something. I'll go back and we'll have another look. We might just see some sign of them."

Jack pulled in and waited for a clear patch in the traffic, before swinging Daisy around and heading back over the ground they'd already covered. Emma felt her pulse racing and her hands getting hot and sweaty.

"We're nearly back into town again and

there's no sign of them," she said, running her fingers through her hair.

"Hey! Over there! There's another horse-box turning into that little side road," yelled Jack. "Let's follow it, Em. Maybe something's going on and old Brunton is there. Chin up, old girl – never give in!"

Jack slipped down the road behind the big green horsebox he'd spotted. Emma felt the road change to a bumpy track beneath them, but kept her eyes fixed on the vehicle ahead.

"Look!" she suddenly squealed, pointing to a little sign pinned to a tree. "It says 'Horse and Pony Auctions'. *That's* where they've gone! That *horrible* Mr Brunton is trying to sell Tuppence, in her state!"

Emma saw the horsebox swing through a metal gate that led into a large field with several marquees in the centre. Cars and horseboxes clustered around them and the place buzzed with activity. Emma felt worried when a man with an official's badge stepped in front of the car.

"Vet." Jack smiled, pointing to the veterinary college sticker on the windscreen.

The man seemed satisfied and waved them on to park.

"Where on earth do we start to look?" sighed Emma. "There are so many horseboxes parked together – lots of horses and ponies being led around and exercised, too."

"Well, we could start by looking amongst the horseboxes, but I reckon Mr Brunton won't have wasted any time. If you're sure he saw you, in town, he'll want to get on with his business and get out of here. Let's begin in the auction tent. I'm going to try and have a word with one of the officials about our Mr Brunton. I want to see that pony isn't sold off to just anyone, in her condition. You wait by the ring and I'll be back in no time."

Emma stood amongst the buyers who were waiting to bid for the horses and ponies about to be led into the ring. Next to her stood a big man in a suit. She thought he stood out from the capped and jacketed figures of the dealers and farmers, who huddled together in groups, muttering to each other. He was puffing and panting in the heat and trying to study the list of horses and ponies up for auction. Emma stood on tiptoe, peering over the heads, hoping to catch a glimpse of the animals waiting to be led in. The auctioneer's voice made her jump as he suddenly spoke into a microphone. But when she looked again and saw the pony being led into the ring she felt her knees go weak. The big dark brown eyes, the gentle face and the rough coat were unmistakable. Emma wanted to cry.

"Tuppence!" she called, but the pony didn't move. Emma thought she looked thin and frail, just standing there for everyone to stare at. Emma was sure someone had given her a bit of a brush before the auction, but that was all.

"I'm going to open the bidding for this four-year-old Welsh pony. A lovely mare. Do I hear two hundred and fifty pounds?"

Emma heard the crowd mumble and the big man in a suit standing next to her laughed.

"Two hundred and fifty pounds! Are they joking?" he said. "She's got a pretty little face, but she's scrawny and grubby. One of her ears is even torn, by the look of it."

Emma heard the auctioneer bring the bidding down to two hundred and then to one hundred pounds. She felt powerless to do anything but feel waves of sympathy for the poor creature, standing shy and obedient by the man who held her rein.

"Oh, where's Jack?" Emma mumbled, trying to spot him amongst the officials.

"Oi, Dad! You buying us a pony, or what?" asked a boy.

Emma yelped as twin boys, about eight years old, pushed past her and trod on her feet. They tugged at the big man's jacket. Emma listened as she heard the one who'd spoken say, "What's wrong with that one in the ring? That'll do. Can't you buy it for us? You *promised* us a pony. Go on, buy it!"

"Do I hear seventy pounds!" Emma heard the auctioneer call.

"If he drops the price by twenty, I'll have her, boys," the big man said.

"Yeah – she'll do. Get her, Dad! We want a ride," pleaded the other boy.

Emma glared at the father and his boys, then shut her eyes, trying to blot out everything.

"Oh, why can't I do anything to stop this – it's all wrong!" she mumbled to herself.

"Do I hear sixty pounds?" called the auctioneer. "*Fifty* then!" he said when there had still been no response.

"Fifty pounds!" bellowed the big man with the boys. He waved his hand in the air. "I'll take her for fifty!"

Emma watched as the auctioneer banged his hand down and spoke into the microphone.

"Sold to the man in the grey suit!"

Emma's heart sank.

"You *can't* buy her," she pleaded with the big man. "She needs care and attention. She's been neglected. Surely you can *see* that? The last thing she needs is your boys jumping about on her."

"Hey, who said they'll jump about on her? I'll look after her, don't you worry, young lady!" said the big man indignantly. "My boys will soon tire of her, anyway. We'll sell her then. She's only for rides at the weekends," he went on, pushing his way over to settle his bid, while his boys tugged at his sleeve.

"We've got a pony!" they chorused. "We've got a pony!"

Emma couldn't believe her eyes as she saw Tuppence being led away from the ring. "If only Jack were here, he could *do* something."

Emma followed the big man and his boys. When the man handed over his money, Emma rushed towards him.

"Look," she began. "I know about that pony and you really are buying yourself an animal that needs a lot of attention. My brother is a vet and he's been treating her. If you take her on you'll be paying out a lot more than fifty pounds. She needs care."

Emma watched the man frown, then look at his unruly twin sons who had begun rolling around on the ground and playfully punching each other.

"I've got forty pounds here," said Emma desperately. "It's all I've got. Why don't you let me buy her from you? If all your boys want is a ride – you could buy them bikes! This is a lovely pony we're talking about, not a piece of machinery or a toy. I promise you everything

I've told you is the truth. Ask my brother – if you'll wait I'll find him."

Emma felt desperate as she watched the man weighing up all she'd said. Then he looked over towards the men who were leading Tuppence into a horsebox and called to them to stop.

"Right," he said turning to Emma. "I'll take your word – and I'll take your money. The *last* thing I need is to buy a load of trouble! I'm a businessman, so I know when someone's offering me a decent deal. And you really are serious about this animal, aren't you?"

"I've never been more serious in my life!" said Emma, handing over the forty pounds she'd taken out of her building society that morning. She shook the man's chubby hand and breathed a sigh of relief when he told his twin sons that the pony deal was off. They stamped their feet in temper and ran off, with their father sweating and panting after them.

Emma felt her head was in a spin. The tent full of mumbling men, the auctioneer's voice, the smell of horses and the reality of what she'd just done made her want to faint.

"Whatever am I going to *do*? I've just bought a *pony*!" Emma muttered to herself. She turned suddenly, at the sound of Jack's voice.

"There you are, Em," puffed Jack, looking very red in the face. "Well, I've had more than a word with that nasty old Brunton – threatened him with getting his farm inspected by the health people. Sorry to say, though, by the time I'd tracked him down, Tuppence had been auctioned and sold. Poor thing, she went for only fifty pounds. I just need to find her new owner and warn whoever it is about Tuppence's condition. Tell them I'm still treating her."

Emma looked uncomfortable.

"Cheer up, Em." Jack continued. "Maybe she's gone to a lovely family who will give her the sort of life she deserves. Someone with a big, warm heart, especially where Tuppence is concerned. Now, let's find that pony's new owner."

Chapter 5

Jack started to move away from the crowded marquee. He stopped when he saw Emma still standing rooted to the spot. "Come on, Em. We've haven't got a minute to lose!"

Emma felt her stomach turn as she plucked up the courage to speak. "There's no need to look any further, Jack. You're looking at the new owner. *I've* just bought Tuppence!"

"This is no time for joking, Emma," Jack said, tugging at his sister's arm.

"But it *isn't* a joke. I really *have* bought Tuppence. I just had to. A big man standing next to me bid for her. He bought her for his two horrible little sons – just as something to ride on at weekends. I gave him my forty pounds for her. *Please* don't be angry. I've no idea what to do next."

Jack let out a deep sigh and frowned at Emma. "You can't just buy an animal like that! What were you thinking? Where do you suppose you're going to keep a Welsh pony at home in London? Perhaps you were thinking of the shed in the back yard at Dad's clinic?"

"I don't know, Jack," sighed Emma. "That's the point, I *wasn't* thinking. I just knew I had to do something! It's like Dad always says, I think with my heart and not my head!"

Jack scratched his thick mop of hair and looked at his watch. "I think I can arrange transport for Tuppence back to Uncle Tim's house. Let's hope he won't mind if we put her in the field behind the house. At least until somewhere is found for her to go. I might just be able to arrange for her to go to a donkey and pony sanctuary. I'll need to make a few phone calls about that. Then maybe, my little sister, I can get down to the work experience I came up here to do!"

*

"Sorry, Uncle," said Emma as she helped Uncle Tim lead Tuppence from the horsebox.

"Well, young Emma, you certainly don't do things by halves," Uncle Tim smiled. "Now let me see. As I recall, you went into town to buy some grooming brushes and horse-feed, and you came back with a pony instead! Tuppence has got to be the biggest animal we've ever had at the sanctuary. But don't worry. I know how you've felt ever since you set eyes on her. We'll arrange something."

Emma was so relieved at the sight of Tuppence standing on safe ground that she wanted to cry.

"Well, Tuppence," she whispered. "This is to be your new home for a very short while, I think. And, although I am your new owner, I really don't know how long that will be for. But while I'm able to live in this dream I'm going to spend every possible minute caring for you."

Tuppence lifted her head and shook her tangled mane.

"Come on," said Uncle Tim. "Let's get her into the field. I need to go and phone over an order for some supplies for the animals. I'll order some hay for Tuppence as well. Meanwhile, there's plenty of fresh grass and a big, tin bath I can fill with water for her to drink," he said.

Uncle Tim stood by while Emma led Tuppence through the gate and untied the leading rein.

"Bit too much for one day, is it?" Emma whispered in Tuppence's ear. "You're free to stretch your legs now," she said.

Emma wondered why the pony didn't move a step, but stayed silently by her side.

"She's taking it all in," said Uncle Tim. "Walk on and see if she follows," he advised.

Emma walked a few paces and looked back to see Tuppence still in the same spot.

"Come on, girl! Come to me," Emma beckoned.

She felt so pleased when Tuppence took a few cautious steps and plodded to her side.

"Good girl – good girl!" Emma said, stroking the side of the pony's face.

"Leave her now, Emma. Let her have a wander around on her own," called Uncle

Tim. "I'm going to go and place that order."

Emma reluctantly left the field and shut the gate, but stayed to look at Tuppence over the top bar. She saw Tuppence move cautiously, further into the field. Then wandering to the far corner, she stopped beneath a big oak tree in the woods where Fred lived. Emma noticed how Tuppence's dark coat blended in with the shadows from the trees.

"Even from here, Tuppence, I can see the light catching your big brown eyes," Emma called. She watched the pony lift her head at the sound, then lower it and begin to nibble at the fresh, green grass. "That's right, Tuppence, you have a feast, but don't make yourself sick. You haven't seen much of that green stuff where you've been living."

Emma turned at the sound of Aunty Margaret's voice.

"Are you coming in for a snack? All the excitement this morning has probably given you an appetite," she said.

"I'm really not very hungry, Aunty," Emma said. "I think it's the excitement that's taken my appetite away! I still can't get my head around the fact that, for a short while, I'll be the owner of the sweetest pony in the world."

"You're right, she is a sweetie," said Aunty Margaret. "With a bit of feeding up and some grooming, I think you'll have a real winner in her."

"I just want Tuppence to go to a good home," said Emma. "I'll feel a lot happier when that's settled. Meanwhile, I mustn't get too attached to her. You know what I'm like about animals – and Tuppence is a very special animal."

"I know *just* what you're like!" laughed Aunty Margaret. "It runs in the family. That's the reason we live here, miles away from anyone, caring for all the poor creatures that come our way."

"Emma!" called Uncle Tim, striding up to them. "You'll be pleased to know that I've just ordered Tuppence some delicious, sweet hay and some decent feed."

"That's great!" said Emma.

"And here's a little something for you. I knew I had it in the shed somewhere. But I can't for the life of me remember why I bought it. Anyway, it's brand new! But let Tuppence settle before you go to work on her poor old coat," Uncle Tim advised.

Emma looked puzzled as she peered into the bag her uncle handed her.

"Oh, Uncle Tim! A grooming brush – brilliant!" she smiled. "I promise I won't wear it out in the next few days."

Emma spent the afternoon wandering to the field and back to check on Tuppence. By standing on the fence and calling to her pony she found Tuppence responded by walking slowly towards her. As she was stepping outside the house for her fourth visit to the field, she saw Jack's car pull up.

"Hi, sis!" he called. "I thought I might just find you out here."

"Tuppence is so sweet. I don't think I'll ever get tired of looking at her. And I want to get as many looks in as possible before she goes."

Emma felt unhappy when she thought about Tuppence going to another owner, before she'd really had a chance to get to know her.

Jack walked with Emma to the field where Tuppence was resting her head over the top of the gate.

"Let's have a look at that ear, young lady," he said to Tuppence. "Very nice – very nice indeed. It's coming along fine," he pronounced. "I've been out on a call with Mr West for the past hour, so I haven't had a chance to contact that donkey and pony sanctuary yet. But you'll be pleased to know that Mr West is going to have some pretty strong words to say to old Brunton, too. What a sneaky man, selling Tuppence off because he thought she was going to cost him."

"Well, his granddaughter obviously wasn't too bothered about her going," said Emma, stroking Tuppence's cheek and inhaling the sweet smell of the pony's warm, damp breath on her cheek. Jack patted Tuppence's neck.

"Come on, Em. I can see the warning signs. You're getting very close to her," said Jack, smiling and leading Emma back to the house. "Now, repeat after me: if I am going to be a good vet I must not get too involved with my patients!"

"But Tuppence isn't my *patient*, Jack. She's my *pony*!" Emma laughed.

Before they reached the door, Aunty Margaret came rushing along the path. "Quick, Jack. An emergency call!"

Jack and Emma broke into a trot.

"What's the problem?" Jack asked, turning towards his car with Aunty Margaret trailing behind.

"Well, it's a dog. It's developed a sudden, nasty cough – like it's choking," Aunty Margaret replied, looking a bit uncomfortable.

"Sounds like it might have swallowed something. Where am I going?" Jack asked, checking his bag was on the back seat.

"This is the bit you're not going to like, Jack," said Aunty Margaret wincing. "You see, the dog belongs to Gloria."

"You're joking! Please say you're joking!" pleaded Jack.

"Poor little dog. Do you want me to come with you?" asked Emma. "I mean, more for you than anything else."

"No thanks, because I'm *not* going! Jack

slammed the car door shut and started to walk back to the house.

"But, Jack, you'll *have* to go – the poor dog's choking," said Aunty Margaret.

Emma watched Jack stop in his tracks and fold his arms across his chest.

"I wouldn't mind betting Gloria has cooked this one up, just to get me over there," he snarled.

"No, honestly. She sounded very distressed on the phone," Aunty Margaret insisted.

Jack sighed loudly.

"Right – *I'll go!*" he said relenting. "But if I'm not back in an hour, send a rescue party for me."

Emma watched as he leapt into the driver's seat. In a moment he had disappeared in a cloud of dust as Daisy rolled off down the track.

"There goes a brave man for you, Aunty," sighed Emma. "Poor old Jack, he came up here to study livestock and he's either sorting out my problems or Gloria Scrumbel's. I'm just going to have one more look at Tuppence for the day. Then I'll stay in and wait for news of my dear brother, who helps all sorts of animals – even ones with long pink claws!" She giggled.

Emma wandered to the edge of the field and saw the beginning of the evening sky taking shape. She scanned the tall grass for Tuppence, but at first she couldn't see her. Eventually, she made out her dark shape under the trees by the edge of the woodland. Tuppence had her head facing into the bushes and Emma thought something was holding her interest. As she looked harder, she saw the figure of a man in a cap stroking Tuppence's side. Something about the way Tuppence was standing made Emma feel sure the pony was content to stand there.

"Fred and Tuppence look just like old friends," she mumbled to herself as she started to walk back to the house.

Then she saw Fred suddenly scale the fence and begin to pat Tuppence's neck. He leaned over and whispered into the pony's ear. Tuppence turned slowly and broke into a gentle trot. Emma's beautiful pony trotted round and round in circles before returning to Fred for praise.

"That was incredible!" Emma exclaimed, awestruck by Fred's special way with animals.

Emma lay in bed looking through an old book she had found in her uncle's study. It was full of information on grooming horses and ponies. She decided she would be up early the next morning to make a start on cleaning Tuppence. As she switched off the light and lay down, still with thoughts of her pony rushing through her head, she heard a knock at the front door. When voices started whispering, she got up and padded to the top of the landing. Looking down, Emma caught sight of Jack leaning with his back against the front door. He was talking to Aunty Margaret. Emma thought he looked exhausted. She could see that Aunty Margaret was embarrassed.

"Jack," Emma whispered. "Are you all right?"

"I suppose you could say I'm all right," Jack called up the stairs. "Especially when you consider I've been savaged by *both* of Gloria's vicious Pekinese dogs. Worst of all, I've barely survived another incident with Gloria!"

"What about the dog, though – the emergency?" Emma asked.

"Well, if Gloria didn't wear long false nails, perhaps little Mitzy wouldn't have choked on one of the wretched things! I got it out without too much of a problem, but Gloria was so appreciative that she insisted on cooking me a meal. The minute she started fussing over me, wanting to take a look at my bad foot, the dogs got jealous."

Emma tried not to giggle, but the thought of Jack fighting off Gloria and the dogs made her want to laugh.

"I never knew Pekinese could be so vicious. Ended up with one hanging by its teeth from my ankle – same foot the cow trod on. The other little brute set about my wrist! But that's not the worst bit, by a long way. Once Gloria had tucked them up in bed, she started on me. It was like a nightmare. I can see it all now – Gloria insisting I finish off my revolting pink dessert, while she proposes *marriage*!"

"She must be *so* desperate!" laughed Emma, while Aunty Margaret tried to look serious.

"Jack," said Aunty Margaret. "I really think it's about time you had a firm word with Gloria and put her well and truly off the scent. Just tell her you already have a girlfriend. I'm sure there must be someone special at home or college."

"That's right," echoed Emma. "It's not a lie. After all, you *do* have a girlfriend – several, actually! Just let her know."

"That's right, be firm! Just tell her next time you see her," advised Aunty Margaret.

"But has anyone ever succeeded in telling Gloria *anything*?" said Jack hopelessly. "Once she's made her mind up – that's it!"

As Emma shut her door she heard her brother saying goodnight to Uncle Tim on the landing.

"By the way, Jack, I can see you need to get some sleep now, but I really want to talk to you about that pony of Emma's. I may have found somewhere for her to go, but I'll tell you in the morning."

As Emma's head hit the pillow, she

wondered what sort of place Uncle Tim had found for Tuppence. She thought how much she trusted her uncle, but all the same, felt desperate to know just what he had in mind.

Chapter 6

"Tuppence!" said Emma, the moment her eyes were open. She jumped out of bed and rushed to the window, but couldn't see the back field from her room. "Never mind," she mumbled to herself. "A quick shower and I'll be with you. No, the shower can wait. I'll have that later on. You're much more important."

Emma pulled on her jeans and the first jumper she laid hands on. Grabbing the grooming brush she rushed downstairs. There was no one about when she tiptoed through the house and let herself out of the front door. She thought the morning air felt crisp when she breathed in and puffed it out in a soft mist that hung around.

Emma found it was still very early. She

climbed on to the fence and scanned the dew-covered field.

"Come, on, Tuppence – my beautiful pony. I've only got a little bit of time left with you. Uncle Tim has found you a home, so please show yourself."

Emma ran the length of the fence, but still couldn't see a trace of the pony. "Oh no! Where are you? I hope you've not got loose!" Then in the very corner of the field she saw Tuppence being led by Uncle Tim – two blurred shapes, the lower parts of their bodies hidden in the mist.

Emma breathed a sigh of relief and called out. "Uncle Tim!" But the figure carried on walking. Emma broke into a run and caught up with them just as they entered the wood through a gap in the trees.

"Emma!" said Uncle Tim, bringing Tuppence to a halt. "You gave me quite a fright. What are you doing up so early? It's only six-thirty, you know."

"I wanted to get started on grooming Tuppence. After all, I won't have her for much longer, will I?"

Her uncle smiled and watched as Emma stroked Tuppence's cheek. "Well, you do have to go back to London and to school, however much we'd love to have you stay. As for Tuppence, I think I've found somewhere perfect for her."

Emma looked into the pony's eyes and saw her own reflection mirrored in the two big circles of light.

"Where, Uncle?" she asked sadly.

"Well, Emma, I'll tell you when I'm absolutely sure about it," he answered. "Perhaps you'd like to join me on a walk to Fred's place. I thought Tuppence might like a stroll through the woods, too. I've some news for Fred about his eviction order."

Emma walked alongside Tuppence and watched her gentle head bobbing as she stepped daintily along the track. In another five minutes Emma saw an old caravan in a clearing and noticed Uncle Tim's expression change. He seemed concerned. "The place looks deserted! The dogs should have barked by now," he said.

Emma looked up as a flutter of birds took

off, as though disturbed by someone in the bushes.

"Look! Over there, Uncle," said Emma, pointing. "Isn't that Fred and his dogs, heading along that overgrown track? He's pushing a pram by the looks of it."

Emma stayed by the caravan holding Tuppence, while Uncle Tim dashed off towards the moving figure. She could see Fred stop in his tracks and the two men talking. Fred shuffled uncomfortably, but eventually he nodded his head, as though agreeing to something. Soon the two men and Fred's big pram, containing all his worldly possessions, headed back along the path. His dogs reached Emma first. She saw how excitable they were and calmed Tuppence by stroking her, in case she was afraid. Emma also noticed that apart from his usual awkward expression, Fred seemed to have a twinkle in his eyes. She thought Uncle Tim had a cheeky grin on his face, too.

"Emma, I'd like you to be the first person to meet my new tenant. Fred will be keeping his caravan in my field from now on. He's going to clear the field and make it his home."

Emma beamed at the two men.

"I knew Tim would care for the animals, so I packed up and set off," Fred said shyly. "Now my caravan's going in the field – marvellous!"

"I suppose you could say Fred and I will be joining forces from now on. We'll be able to take on more animal cases by working together."

"That's brilliant, Uncle. I'm so pleased for you, Fred. I'd have hated to see you thrown out of your home."

"Your uncle was kind enough to ask me to live in the house and it's not that I'm ungrateful for such a generous offer, but I'm used to the outdoors now," said Fred. "Anyway, I'll be having someone special to share the field with me. So my first job will be to tidy it up."

Emma looked puzzled and wondered who Fred was talking about. She continued to wonder when she led Tuppence back into the field and Fred showed her some tips on grooming.

*

An hour later Jack looked over the fence and called to Emma.

"Hey, little sister! No time to talk to me these days?"

Emma led Tuppence over to him. "Excuse me," he said. "But am I right in assuming this is the very same pony that you rescued from the Brunton family?"

Emma stood back and joined Jack in admiring the way Tuppence looked. She felt pleased her efforts had made such a difference.

"I've used the brush Uncle Tim gave me. She does look good, doesn't she? Fred has sorted out her mane and it looks so alive now." Emma thought Tuppence looked dazzling.

"Fred is going to see to her hooves later. She's a real winner, don't you think?" Emma smiled. "Just a shame I couldn't have kept her somehow. Have *you* any idea about the new home Uncle Tim has found for her? I overheard him telling you last night that he'd let you know."

"Listening in, were you?" Jack smiled, tweaking her ear. "Well, I'm not one for gossip – just a vet in training, here to inspect my patient's poor ear. Come on, Tuppence, show me that furry thing at the top of your head."

Jack climbed on to the fence to examine the pony's ear. "Ah, yes," he said, congratulating himself. "Another piece of first-class workmanship from the hands of Jack Hodges – rising young star in the veterinary world. It's coming along nicely. No sign of infection there," he said climbing down. "Well, I can't stop here chatting to you when I have calls to make. The delights of Mr and Mrs Slackshaw's prize ram await me on their farm. I'm assisting Mr West there this morning. He's pleased with me, you know."

Emma watched Jack strut off down the path and called after him.

"You never know, Jack, he might offer you a place in his practice when you qualify. Just think, you could settle down with Gloria then!" Emma laughed.

Jack pulled a horrible face. "By the way," he called. "You'll be pleased to know that I've given Uncle Tim a list of stuff that I think might help Tuppence's condition – vitamins and all that. He should be seeing a real improvement in the weeks to come."

"Great!" called Emma and returned to her brushing. "Did you hear that?" she whispered in Tuppence's ear. "Uncle Tim will be giving you some lovely food and. . ." Emma broke off, suddenly aware of Jack's words. "Why did he say *Uncle Tim* would be helping to get Tuppence back into shape again, if he's found somewhere for her to live?"

Emma found her uncle in one of the sheds, preparing feeds for the badger and the fox. She loved the way everything for the animals was kept labelled, and securely stored, in old ice-cream containers. Nothing in Aunty Margaret's kitchen ever went to waste. Uncle Tim was forever telling her not to throw things away because he could find a use for them in the sheds.

"Uncle Tim," said Emma. "I was wondering if you could tell me yet where Tuppence will be going to live. I'm just bursting to know, if you're sure now."

Emma's uncle looked up from the bowl of food he was mixing and Emma saw a mischievous look in his eyes. "Well, I was going to keep it as a bit of a surprise for you, Emma, but I've got a sneaky feeling you have an idea that it won't be *too* far away from me."

Emma's eyes grew wider.

"Come with me," said Uncle Tim. "I'm going to feed the fox."

Emma tried to conceal her impatience to discover what her uncle had in mind for Tuppence. She waited while he put out food for the fox.

"Come on, foxy!" he called, as a pair of inquisitive golden brown eyes stared at him from the back of the run. "Now Emma, do you remember hearing Fred say he was going to be sharing the field with another lodger?

"Yes," Emma replied. "I've been wondering who it will be."

"Well, it's a female. She's got dark hair, big brown eyes with thick lashes and skinny legs – but it's *not* Gloria! Any guesses?" Uncle Tim's face broke into the biggest smile Emma thought she'd ever seen.

Emma almost knocked the food bowls over as she rushed at Uncle Tim, throwing her arms around his neck.

"You are the *greatest*! Thank you!" she squealed.

"Steady on, old girl. You'll frighten the fox!" he said. "Your pony will have to earn her keep here, you know. I got to thinking about when she's really fit and healthy again. She can come with us to some of the local shows and help promote the different animal charities we support."

"That's *wonderful*, Uncle Tim," said Emma. "I bet she'll be so popular."

"Of course I'll give her plenty of time to get used to being around people first," Uncle Tim assured Emma. "I'm sure the children will love fussing over her – providing her owner agrees. After all, I would imagine *she* will be paying her pony quite a few visits in the years to come. She might even take up riding herself. What do you think?"

Chapter 7

Emma spent almost every second of the rest of the week close to Tuppence. She felt so overwhelmed by all that had happened. At last it was time to go. While Jack packed their cases in the boot of his beloved Daisy, Emma said goodbye to Tuppence.

"Who would have thought that I'd have bought my own pony? Who, I might add, just happens to be the most wonderful pony that ever trotted the earth," she whispered into Tuppence's ear, as the pony munched on a piece of apple Emma had given her. "Well, Tuppence, my beauty, I'm leaving you now, but I promise I'll be back soon."

Emma kissed the top of the pony's head and

patted her neck. She didn't feel sad at leaving – just peaceful.

"Come on, Em, we need to get on the road. The speed old Daisy travels means it'll be the early hours of the morning before I deliver you back to Mum and Dad. Just wait until they hear you've bought a *pony*!"

"Thank you, Aunty and Uncle, for having me to stay. I'm sorry I seem to have left you with all the responsibility of caring for Tuppence," Emma said.

"And I can't think of a more welcome responsibility to have," laughed Uncle Tim. "Now you be on your way."

"And be sure to ring and let us know you got home safely," Aunty Margaret smiled, handing Emma a bag full of food for the return journey.

Emma kissed everyone goodbye and sat in the front of the car. Just as Jack started the engine, Fred ran down the track from the field. Emma could see he was carrying something heavy in his arms.

"These are for you, Emma," he said shyly. "I

bought them a long time ago. They need a lot of work on them, but when you come back to us again, I'll have restored them."

Emma stared at the lovely old leather saddle and bridle in Fred's arms.

"Thank you Fred," she said, feeling tears of happiness welling up. "I just know that you and Tuppence are going to have a great time sharing the field. She likes you. I've seen how comfortable she feels around you. I've seen you talking to her."

Fred blushed. "I suppose I do have a bit of a way with the animals, whatever their size. I reckon we speak the same language," he said, staring at the ground.

Fred joined Aunty Margaret and Uncle Tim, as Jack stuck an arm out of the window and waved as they bounced off down the drive. As the little car gained speed, Emma turned for a last look at Tuppence, who was staring over the fence from the field. The light caught the sheen on her coat and Emma saw her toss her head and trot off to the other side of the field.

"You've bought a lovely animal, there,

Em," smiled Jack. "And some vet, who obviously knew his stuff, did a good job on her ear!"

Emma looked behind her once more at the farmhouse, disappearing into the distance, as Jack came to a halt at the main road. Aunty Margaret, Uncle Tim and Fred were only little figures in the huge landscape, but they were still waving. Emma knew that not far behind them, Tuppence would still be stretching her legs or eating the sweet hay that had been delivered.

As the little car pulled out, Emma heard Jack gasp and his foot hit the brake. "*Gloria!*"

Emma watched the vision in pink sweep out of her Mini, which she'd driven across Jack's path to block him. She wobbled up to the car and thrust her face in at Jack's window.

"You mean to say you were *leaving* without saying a word to me? When will you be back, Jack? Distance can't keep us apart for long, you know!"

Emma wriggled uncomfortably as Jack struggled for words. "I've left you a letter, Gloria. It explains everything," he said, looking serious and hanging his head. "I'm afraid there's another female in my life."

Gloria put her hand to her mouth in shock and staggered back to her car.

As Jack's car eventually gained speed, Emma turned to look at the pink figure, still teetering on spindly heels by her car. Emma thought how much the colour pink looked strangely out of place amongst the lush greens and coppers of the peaks.

"So, Jack, who *is* the other female in your life?"

Jack grinned and winked at Emma.

"You're sitting in her – Daisy, of course. It's the truth!"

Emma had been back at school for six weeks when the morning post fell on the mat at the Handley Road Veterinary Clinic. She had been making lots of phone calls to Uncle Tim and Aunty Margaret to ask how Tuppence was getting on. They had insisted that she spend a weekend with them soon. "After all, your pony needs you to come and exercise her," Uncle Tim had said.

Emma opened the letter. She recognized Uncle Tim's handwriting and lingered over every word:

Dear Emma,

Here is a photograph of Tuppence at one of the local shows. I don't expect you can see much of the lovely old saddle and bridle Fred restored, because there are so many children gathered around her. Wherever we take her she seems to draw the crowds! We really hope it won't be long before you come to stay again. After all, your pony needs you to keep her exercised.

Lots of love, for now,
Uncle Tim.

Emma stared at the picture of Tuppence surrounded by lots of happy-faced children. She still couldn't believe that this was the pony she'd first seen at the Bruntons' farm. In the photograph Tuppence looked fit and healthy. Her coat shone and she had put on weight. Emma thought she still had that shy look which would always be a special part of her.

"I can't believe how well you look," she whispered to the photograph. "But most of all – I still can't believe you belong to me."

Emma rushed upstairs to find her mum and dad. They hadn't seen her pony yet.